Queen Munch
and Queen Nibble

For Ella, with love from Mummy – C. D.

To Madeleine – L. M.

First published in 2002 by Macmillan Children's Books
A division of Macmillan Publishers Limited
20 New Wharf Road, London N1 9RR
Basingstoke and Oxford
Associated companies throughout the world
www.panmacmillan.com

ISBN 0 333 96065 3 (HB)
ISBN 0 333 96066 1 (PB)

Text copyright © 2002 Carol Ann Duffy
Illustrations copyright © 2002 Lydia Monks
Moral rights asserted.

1 3 5 7 9 8 6 4 2

A CIP catalogue record for this book is available
from the British Library.

Printed in China

nesta

*Carol Ann Duffy gratefully acknowledges a Fellowship from NESTA.
NESTA – the National Endowment for Science, Technology and the Arts –
was set up in 1998 to support innovation and creative potential in the UK.*

Queen Munch and Queen Nibble

by Carol Ann Duffy   *illustrated by* Lydia Monks

MACMILLAN CHILDREN'S BOOKS

Queen Munch was big with cheeks as red as tomato ketchup. She had shining ginger hair which she wore in two plump pigtails like strings of Best Sausages. Her eyes were the colour of chutney and her laugh was as loud and as deep as the moo of a cow on its way to be milked.

She always wore a crown: a plain diamond one for weekdays and the Great Ruby Crown for the weekends. She wore purple or orange or scarlet frocks (she never called them dresses) and each one took six sewing maids seven Sundays to stitch.

Queen Munch lived in Munch Palace, which looked a bit like a wedding cake. Her people loved her and every Saturday morning they would come by bus, bike or donkey to watch The Munching of the Breakfast.

First of all the three Servants of the Queen's Kitchen would march onto the Palace balcony with a round polished table and a red velvet chair, with the best china and cutlery and a solid silver teapot. The people would stare and point and talk excitedly as spoons and knives and forks glinted high up on the balcony.

Suddenly the Royal Musicians would appear behind the Palace Gates and even the youngest child there would know that soon they would be playing the Queen Munch Tune. There were no words to this tune but it was lively and jazzy, with trumpets and clarinets and banjos, and no one with ears on each side of their head could hear it without wanting to dance.

The Royal Musicians would shout 1, 2, 3, 4! and then swing into the music, the whole crowd would start to hop and boogie, babies would bounce up and down in their prams and such a wonderful time would be had by one and all

that, by the time Queen Munch danced onto the balcony and plumped herself down on the red velvet chair, the joint was jumping!

When the Musicians had finished playing, with a final, happy yell from the trumpet, the three Servants would begin to serve the Queen her breakfast from a trolley sparkling with gold and silver plates and bowls. At the same time the Royal Cook would walk shyly onto the balcony in her white chef's hat next to the Important Reader of the Menu. Boys and girls looked at everything with

wishing eyes – the endless blue sky with its fluffy clouds like meringues, the yummy-looking Palace, the jewels like boiled sweets in the Great Ruby Crown on the Queen's head . . . and then they would hear the big, booming, posh voice of the Important Reader as he read out the Menu for that Saturday's Munching of the Breakfast.

"Hear ye! Pay attention! Listen up! Here is the Menu for the Breakfast of Her Majesty Queen Munch the Third, on Saturday the Twelveteen of Summer, Two Thousand and Nice."

The Important Reader would pause then and look out at the silent, tender crowd. Sometimes a baby would cry until it was shooshed by its mummy or a little girl would accidentally let go of her yellow balloon and watch it float away into the blue air forever.

"Three poached eggs from the Golden Goose!" shouted the Important Reader.

"Aaaah!" said the crowd.

"Toast cut up into soldiers!"

"Mmmmmmm!" hummed the crowd.

"One grilled prize-winning tomato from the Royal Greenhouse!"

"Oooh!"

"Five fried mushrooms picked fresh this morning from a Fairy Circle!"

"Yummmmm!"

Every child, woman and man in the crowd would be licking their lips by now as Queen Munch munched away on her balcony. Then they would begin to cheer and wave their pink and turquoise paper flags. Queen Munch would put down her teacup, belch loudly and get to her feet.

"Hurrah!" the crowd would roar. "Hurrah! Hurrah!"

"I'm really really really full now," Queen Munch would say. She would pat her tummy and look happily down at the huge crowd below, the hundreds of flags shivering like flowers in a breeze.

She could see the town behind everyone, the churches and houses and schools and shops just as splendid as gingerbread. And beyond the town was the edge of the Big Dark Forest which separated Queen Munch's Queendom from Queen Nibble's.

Queen Nibble! What was she like? Was she fun? Did she like to laugh and bounce up and down on her mattress? Could she play Snap and shout "SNAP!" at the top of her voice if she won?

It was on a Saturday morning just like any other that Queen Munch first had the clever idea
of inviting Queen Nibble
to visit.

Queen Nibble was as tall and slender and pale as a stick of celery. She liked to wear only pale colours – white or beige or light grey – so all her dresses were hung out to dry at night by the light of the moon. Today she was wearing a delicate white dress with pale blue lacy bits like a winter sky.

She wore her fine fair hair up in a tidy bundle the size of a white bread roll. A simple pearl tiara, like a row of tiny pickled onions, sat on her head.

She lived alone in the Long Tower of Nibble Castle and would only let one Servant wait on her. (This was Goodnurse Scrubadub who had babysat Queen Nibble since she was two.)

The one thing that made Queen Nibble really happy was making rain jewellery. Only a real Queen was able to do this. When it rained she would rush outside, pull her long silver needle from one pocket and her golden thread from another and run up and down, threading and stitching the rain as it fell.

She made wonderful necklaces from the rain, beautiful earrings and pretty rings, fabulous tiaras and twinkling cufflinks. This amazing jewellery was kept under guard in Nibble Castle in a glass case which read:

JEWELS FROM THE RAIN OF QUEEN NIBBLE

and nobody was allowed to touch it.

But it wasn't
raining today. Queen Nibble
stared out from her window at the
Big Dark Forest. Her eyes were as
green as slices of cucumber. In her
thin hand she held the invitation
from the Queen who lived on the
other side of the trees. Queen
Munch. It was forbidden for one
Queen to say "No" to an invitation
from another Queen, so she knew
she must go. But she didn't want to.

"You'll enjoy it when you get there," said Goodnurse Scrubadub, as she dunked a nettle teabag into Queen Nibble's cup of hot water. "What would you like to eat with this tonight?"

Queen Nibble thought about this. She wasn't hungry. In fact, she was never hungry, but she knew she'd better ask for something. "I think I want an olive," she said. "A green olive."

"With chips?" asked Goodnurse Scrubadub, hopefully.

"No chips. Just an olive. Thank you. I hope I shan't have to eat a lot when I visit Queen Munch."

"She'll have a party for you," said Goodnurse Scrubadub. "There will be jelly and crisps and little sausages on sticks and pizza and ice cream. I'm looking forward to going!"

Queen Nibble wasn't looking forward to going at all.

But that night, as Queen Nibble lay in her bed looking up through the window at the moon, which was busy drying her colourless dresses, she thought about Queen Munch. She wondered what she would be like and if perhaps, after all, it might be nice to have a friend.

I hope she likes the rain, thought Queen Nibble. I hope she likes to sit peacefully like a cat at a window. I hope she likes to watch the mist wind around the forest like a ribbon. Then Queen Nibble fell asleep and lay as still as a cold white statue.

Far away, on the other side of the Big Dark Forest, Queen

Munch snorted and snuffled and snored, dreaming happily

of the new Queen who was coming to visit her.

The next morning Queen Nibble set off through the forest on her white llama, wearing her palest dress and cloak and the North Pole Crown, which had been carved from ice by her great-great-great-great grandmother and could never melt. Goodnurse Scrubadub walked beside the llama holding the bridle.

Sometimes Goodnurse Scrubadub asked Queen Nibble a question, or pointed to one of the colourful lollipop-birds who lived in the forest, or started to sing a bit of a song . . . but Queen Nibble stayed as quiet as a mushroom.

Then Goodnurse Scrubadub said they must stop for a rest and a snack so they sat down under the shade of an Umbrella Tree, listening to the lollipop-birds licking their red and green wings in the branches. Queen Nibble nibbled a green grape and refused to eat any of the crisps or sandwiches.

Goodnurse Scrubadub fed and watered the llama and they went on their way.

As they began to reach the other side of the Big Dark Forest they noticed that someone had been tying balloons onto all the trees, pink balloons, turquoise balloons, and as they walked through the town they saw that every house was covered in flags. Queen Nibble pulled her hood up.

Then they heard a funny noise, like lots of bees making honey, and looked up and saw Munch Palace on the hill with a huge crowd outside it.

"Goodness!" said Goodnurse Scrubadub.

When the crowd saw tall, pale, thin, cloaked-and-hooded Queen Nibble coming silently towards them on her white llama they went very quiet, as though each and every one of them had been told off.

Goodnurse Scrubadub, head held high in her best nurse's uniform, saw the crowd part before her and she squeezed tightly at the llama's bridle and led Queen Nibble into the Palace courtyard.

In front of them was an enormous cream cake the size of a cottage. Queen Nibble got off her llama, pulled back her hood and stared at it. The crowd behind her held its breath.

All at once the Royal Musicians came marching out from behind the giant cake. Doodle-oodle-oodle-oo! yodelled the trumpet. It was the Queen Munch Tune! A stable boy ran up and led away the llama and the Important Reader could be seen striding towards Queen Nibble and her Nurse. But where was Queen Munch?

The Important Reader was bowing now, first to Queen Nibble and then to Goodnurse Scrubadub, who blushed like a blancmange as he bent to kiss her hand. The Musicians played their last joyful chord.

"Look!" squawked a girl in the crowd with a face like a parrot. "Look!"

The lid of the cake flew back, spattering dollops of cream everywhere like snowballs, and Queen Munch jumped out of the inside of the cake and landed SLAP! in front of Queen Nibble. She was wearing the Great Ruby Crown and a MASSIVE smile. Queen Nibble looked like a ghost on a diet.

"Welcome!" yelled Queen Munch. "Welcome to our new friend, Queen Nibble!"

"Hip hip hop hop hurrah!" roared the crowd.

Queen Munch grabbed hold of Queen Nibble's hand as if it was an empty glove. "Come on in!" she cried, and pulled her new friend into the Palace.

"So!" said Queen Munch. "How's about a slap-up tea and then I'll race you round the Royal Gardens?"

But Queen Nibble wasn't tempted by any of the food the courtiers offered, not even the Royal Orchard Trifle, which had real hummingbirds and rare butterflies hovering and fluttering around it.

When she couldn't refuse any more, she whispered, "A quiet stroll round the gardens might be nice."

"Fabaroony," said Queen Munch, and raced for the gate. Queen Nibble tip-toed behind her.

They had just set foot outside when . . . Plop!

Queen Munch jumped. Plip-plop!

Queen Nibble looked up at the sky. Drip-drop!

Plip-plip-plip! Plop-plop-plop!

Drip! Drop! Drip-drip! Drop! Drop!

"IT'S RAINING!" thundered Queen Munch.

If there was one thing Queen Munch couldn't stand it was rain. Whenever it rained she would go to bed for the rest of the day and sit there wearing her nightdress and a rainhat and clutching a huge umbrella.

"It's only a summer shower, Your Majesty," whispered the Important Reader, but Queen Munch was having none of it.

"I'm off to bed," she said, and she turned to go back inside.

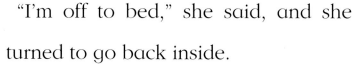

But Queen Nibble had pulled her long silver needle from one pocket and her golden thread from another and had started on a small bracelet.

"Look!" gasped the Very Important Reader. "She's making jewellery from the rain!"

"It's a special talent," said Goodnurse Scrubadub proudly. Queen Munch stopped in her tracks. She stared excitedly as Queen Nibble darted to and fro until the beautiful raindrop bracelet was finished and glittering in her palm like treasure from Heaven.

The two Queens faced each other in the soft rain and Queen Munch held out her plump pink wrist for Queen Nibble to fasten the bracelet around it.

Suddenly Queen Munch didn't want to go to her bed any more. Yes, it was raining – BUT SHE DIDN'T REALLY CARE!

"Can I have a go?" she asked, looking with gleaming Queen eyes at the silver needle and the golden thread.

"Certainly," said Queen Nibble in her pale, quiet voice, and she gave them to her.

"Oh!" gasped the Very Important Reader.

"Ah!" beamed Goodnurse Scrubadub.

Queen Munch poked at a fat raindrop with the needle.

She laughed with delight as it wobbled onto the golden thread like a pearl. She trotted here and there, jabbing and prodding, threading and looping, just as Queen Nibble had, until she had made a very wonky (but still gorgeous) brooch from the tumbling rain. She pinned it to Queen Nibble's colourless dress where it shone like the moon in a puddle. Goodnurse Scrubadub clapped her hands with pleasure and the Important Reader winked at her. It stopped raining. The sun beamed down like a best friend.

The next day, Queen Munch burst into Queen Nibble's dressing room wearing a new frock that was covered all over in pretend strawberries, cherries, gooseberries, raspberries and kumquats.

"Fancy playing a game?" she yelled.

Queen Nibble did not fancy playing a game at all, but it was forbidden for one Queen to refuse to play a game with another Queen so she knew she had to. Meekly, she followed Queen Munch to the front of the palace.

A huge crowd was waiting and Queen Nibble turned paler than ever.

"I thought I'd invite everyone," said Queen Munch. "Now, do you see this frock?"

Queen Nibble nodded.

"Well, one – and only one – of these fruits is real. If you can guess which one it is then you can eat it."

Queen Nibble looked over at Goodnurse Scrubadub for help but she was busy giggling away with the Important Reader. "All right," she said, in a voice as small as an apple pip.

"But I'm not hungry."

"I know. You never are," said Queen Munch, putting her arm around Queen Nibble. She smells like trifle, thought Queen Nibble, but I don't seem to mind. Queen Munch gave a loud sniff. She smells like the rain, she thought, how splendid. "But listen to me. *If* you find the only real fruit on this frock and *if* you eat it, then you will have a wonderful, healthy, yumaroony appetite for the rest of your puff. What could be better than that?"

Queen Nibble could see her own reflection in each of Queen Munch's friendly chutney eyes. She looked like a candle without a flame. Queen Munch snapped her fingers at the Important Reader like castanets. He let go of Goodnurse Scrubadub's toasty hand and clicked his shiny, seaside-rock-coloured boots together.

"Hear ye! Pay attention! Listen up! Their Majesties Queen Munch and Queen Nibble will now play Find the Fruit on the Frock!"

"Ooooooo!" sang the crowd, as though they were getting in tune.

"Queen Nibble has agreed to try to find the only real fruit on Queen Munch's dress and to eat it if she finds it."

"Aaaaaah!" gasped the crowd.

The Royal Drummer started to thump his drum like a heartbeat as Queen Munch spread her arms in the sunshine and Queen Nibble began to walk slowly around her. The Great Ruby Crown and the North Pole Crown seemed to throw handfuls of light between each other like silver coins into a hat. Goodnurse Scrubadub found that she'd linked arms with the Important Reader. A small boy with ginger hair giggled in the crowd and was clipped round the ear by a priest. Every single heart there was beating in time with the drum. Badabum. Badabum. Badabum.

Queen Nibble reached out and plucked a strawberry from Queen Munch's frock.

"Wuufffff!" went the crowd, drawing in its breath like a bicycle pump.

Queen Nibble popped the strawberry into her mouth with all the courage of a true Queen. She bit down hard with her teeth. Queen Munch hopped up and down with excitement like an orchard in the wind. The drumming stopped and suddenly there was silence.

Queen Nibble chewed. Her mouth filled with juice, the juice of summer and sunshine and silliness, a pink tingling juice that put pictures into her mind of balloons and wobbling red jellies and a best friend with a big daft laugh. The juice trickled down her chin and onto her palest dress, staining it forever in a shape exactly like a heart.

Queen Nibble looked at Queen Munch and realised that she was Absolutely Starving!

"She's done it!" shrieked Queen Munch. "IT'S THE REAL ONE!"

After that no one could ever remember exactly what happened. The crowd started to throw bananas in the air, the Musicians started to play a song called Wild Queen Blues, and Goodnurse Scrubadub and the Important Reader danced over every stone in the Palace courtyard. Queen Munch juggled with the pretend kumquats off her frock and Queen Nibble laughed so hard that the North Pole Crown started to melt and had to be put into the Royal Fridge by the Royal Cook.

Then Queen Munch ordered a Town Feast and out came the Town Table which was half a mile long and everyone sat down and the Royal Cook roasted and grilled and steamed and stirred and the Servants of the Queen's Kitchen ran up and down with plates of food the likes of which had not been seen since Queen Munch was crowned.

The two Queens sat at either end of the table and Queen Munch munched away and Queen Nibble nibbled away and

Goodnurse Scrubadub looked on proudly as the Important Reader of the Menu strutted his stuff. But everyone was far too busy eating to listen.

From that day onwards, Queen Nibble visited Queen Munch for six months of every year. In honour of Queen Nibble, Queen Munch declared that any day it rained was to be a National Holiday from work and from school.

Children who crept up to the Palace in the evenings, when the moon had just started to smile in the pale pink sky, could hear the two Queens playing Snap on the balcony. Sometimes they would see their shadows behind the curtains, bouncing on Queen Munch's enormous bed. Queen Munch bounced highest but Queen Nibble could always bounce for longer.

And the girl who looked like a parrot said that she had once seen them float off from the Palace roof in a hot air balloon . . . but no one believed her.

Goodnurse Scrubadub and the Important Reader swapped rings and agreed that they would be married one day, but not just yet.

And, of course, for the other six months of the year Queen Munch went to visit Queen Nibble in Nibble Castle. But that's another story.

Now . . . what would *you*

like for breakfast in the morning?